Written by P.E. Barnes and

Illustrated by Cameron Wilson

Dedication

This book is dedicated to all the game changers in the world.

Ben owns a successful video gaming company.

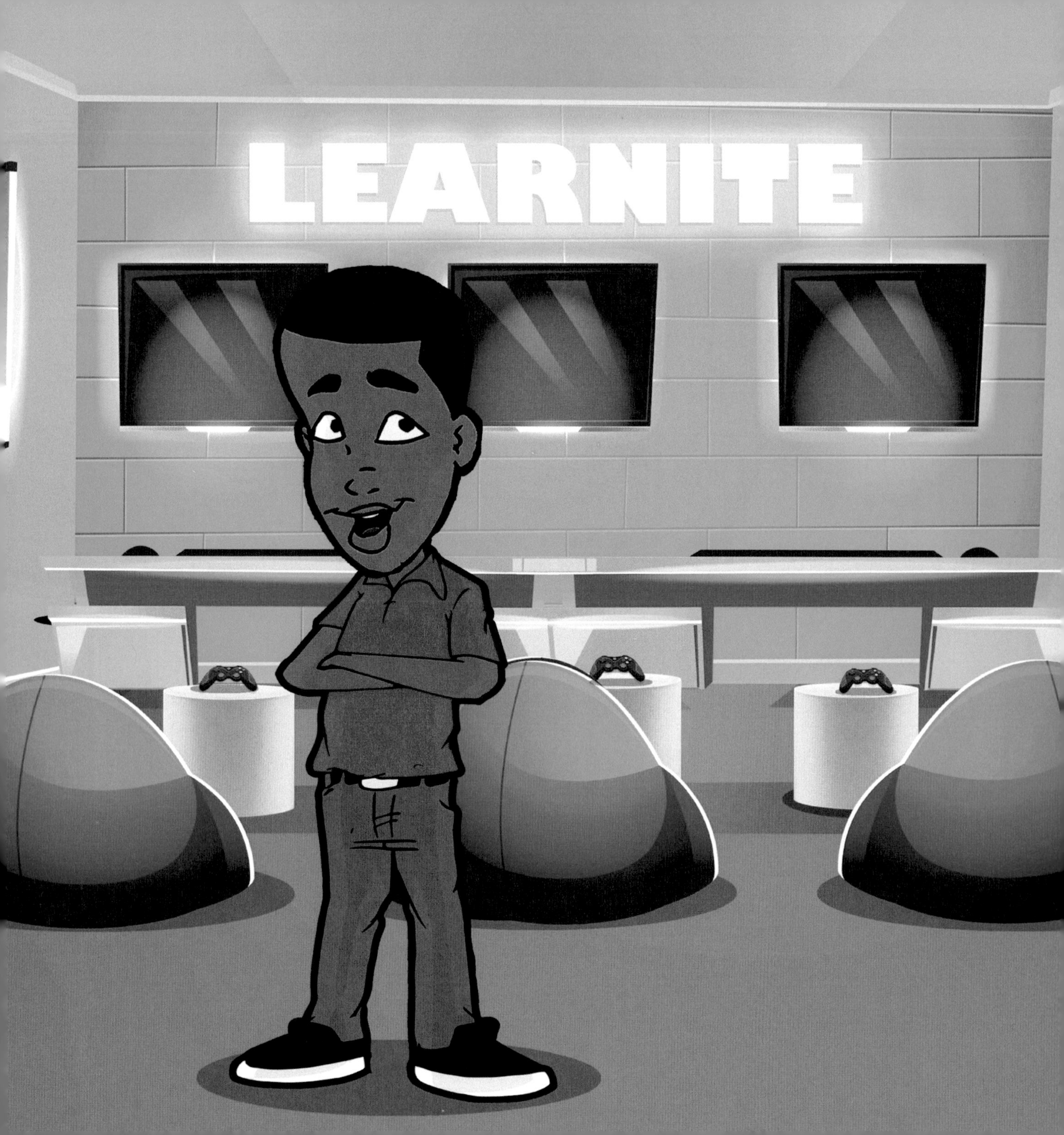
LEARNITE

Ben started working with computers and gaming at a young age.

Ben excelled in his Information Technology class in school. His teacher encouraged his mom to enroll him in coding classes.

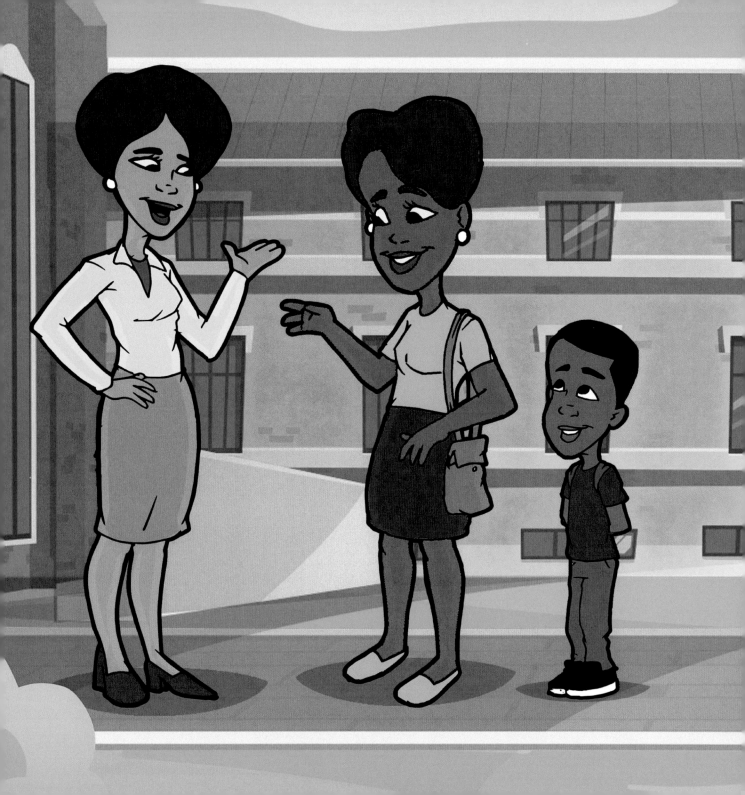

Ben loved the coding class, he learned so many new things he could do with a computer. He became the computer expert at school.

Ben learned to build websites and began working on building apps for his friends to communicate with each other.

He graduated from high school and went to college and there he began to work with other students studying computer engineering.

Ben loved to play his game system competitively with his friends on the weekends, he began working on inventing his own competitive game.

After months of working on the game

and getting input from his peers, he

was ready to test the game out with

his friends. He named the game

Learnite.

His friends loved the game, Learnite, they wanted to know how they could get their own copy to play in the dorm. Ben began to distribute the game to his friends, family and eventually he began to sell it to the public.

Ben started to receive million dollar offers to buy his company. He declined the offers and maintained ownership and grew his company to a billion dollars.

The End

S.T.E.M

SCIENCE, TECHNOLOGY, ENGINEERING, AND MATHEMATICS

What is computer coding? Coding is the process of using a programming language to get a computer to behave how you want it to.

What is information technology? The use of computers to store, retrieve, transmit, and change data or information.

Educating children to become the innovators and inventors of tomorrow begins with STEM. The skill set of this century's careers include media and technology literacy, social skills, communication, flexibility and initiative. STEM education includes problem solving, critical thinking, creativity, curiosity, decision making, leadership, entrepreneurship, and more.

GAMING AND APP GOALS

About the Author

P.E. Barnes is a real estate investor in Chicago. She is passionate about educating children about financial literacy. She is a wife and mother of two young boys that inspired this book series.

For bookings or inquiries email: littleowners@gmail.com

Made in the USA
Monee, IL
27 July 2020